The Dancing Dog

Written by Jasmin Glynne
Illustrated by Pat Murray

 Collins

The dancing dog can do the tango.
Step, slide, tappity tap.

2

The dancing dog can do tap.
Step, slide, tappity tap.

The dancing dog can do ballet.
Step, slide, tappity tap.

The dancing dog can do street dance.
Step, slide, tappity tap.

The dancing dog can do ballroom.

Step ...

Slip!

The dancing dog can't do ballroom.

The Dancing Dog's Dance School

tango

tap

ballet

street dance

ballroom

Ideas for guided reading

Learning objectives: find specific information in simple texts; tell stories and describe incidents from their own experience in an audible voice; retell stories, ordering events using story language; build new stores of words to communicate in different contexts; create short simple texts on paper that combine words with images

Curriculum links: Music: Ongoing skills; PE: Dance activities

High frequency words: the, can, do, can't

Interest words: tango, tap, ballet, street dance, ballroom

Word count: 68

Resources: instruments, whiteboard, drawing materials

Getting started

- Ask children if they like dancing and encourage them to tell stories from their own experiences. *When do you dance? Who with?*

- Read the blurb, including the question "How many dances can he do?" and ask children to look out for these when they read the book.

- Tell the children that this is a poem and ask them what they think a poem is. Discuss the features of rhythm and rhyme, and explain that poems can have both or neither. Ask children to look out for what features this book has.

Reading and responding

- Read the first page together and emphasise the rhythm of "step, slide, tappity tap". Encourage children to recite and remember this.

- Ask children to read on independently to the end. Support struggling readers, praising and prompting them where necessary.

- Discuss how the dog felt when he fell over, similar embarrassing moments the children might have had, and how they dealt with them.